P. D. JAMES

THE GIRL WHO
LOVED GRAVEYARDS
AND
THE VICTIM

D1393320

PENGUIN BOOKS

PENGUIN BOOKS

Published by the Penguin Group. Penguin Books Ltd, 27 Wrights Lane, London w8 5TZ, England. Penguin Books USA Inc., 375 Hudson Street, New York, New York 10014, USA. Penguin Books Australia Ltd, Ringwood, Victoria, Australia. Penguin Books Canada Ltd, 10 Alcorn Avenue, Toronto, Ontario, Canada M4V 3B2. Penguin Books (NZ) Ltd, 182–190 Wairau Road, Auckland 10, New Zealand · Penguin Books Ltd, Registered Offices: Harmondsworth, Middlesex, England · The two stories – 'The Victim' first published 1973; 'The Girl Who Loved Graveyards' first published as 'A Childhood Obsession' in *Living*, August 1989 – in this edition published 1996 · Copyright © P. D. James 1973, 1989 · All rights reserved · Typeset by Rowland Phototypesetting Ltd, Bury St Edmunds, Suffolk. Printed in England by Clays Ltd, St Ives plc · Except in the United States of America, this book is sold subject to the condition that it shall not, by way of trade or otherwise, be lent, re-sold, hired out, or otherwise circulated without the publisher's prior consent in any form of binding or cover other than that in which it is published and without a similar condition including this condition being imposed on the subsequent purchaser · 10 9 8 7 6 5 4 3 2 1

CONTENTS

The Victim

You know Princess Ilsa Mancelli, of course. I mean
by that that you must have seen her on the cinema
screen; on television; pictured in newspapers arriving
at airports with her latest husband; relaxing on their
yacht; bejewelled at first nights, gala nights, at any
night and in any place where it is obligatory for the
rich and successful to show themselves. Even if, like
me, you have nothing but bored contempt for what I
believe is called the international jet set, you can hardly
live in the modern world and not know Ilsa Mancelli.
And you can't fail to have picked up some scraps about
her past. The brief and not particularly successful
screen career, when even her heartstopping beauty
couldn't quite compensate for the paucity of talent;
the succession of marriages, first to the producer who
made her first film and who broke a twenty-year-old
marriage to get her; then to a Texan millionaire; lastly
to a prince. About two months ago I saw a nauseatingly
sentimental picture of her with her two-day-old son
in a Rome nursing home. So it looks as if this marriage,

sanctified as it is by wealth, a title and maternity, may be intended as her final adventure.

The husband before the film producer is, I notice, no longer mentioned. Perhaps her publicity agent fears that a violent death in the family, particularly an unsolved violent death, might tarnish her bright image. Blood and beauty. In the early stages of her career they hadn't been able to resist that cheap, vicarious thrill. But not now. Nowadays her early history, before she married the film producer, has become a little obscure, although there is a suggestion of poor but decent parentage and early struggles suitably rewarded. I am the most obscure part of that obscurity. Whatever you know, or think you know of Ilsa Mancelli, you won't have heard about me. The publicity machine has decreed that I be nameless, faceless, unremembered, that I no longer exist. Ironically, the machine is right; in any real sense, I don't.

I married her when she was Elsie Bowman aged seventeen. I was assistant librarian at our local branch library and fifteen years older, a thirty-two-year-old virgin, a scholar manqué, thin faced, a little stooping, my meagre hair already thinning. She worked on the cosmetic counter of our High Street store. She was beautiful then, but with a delicate, tentative unsophisticated loveliness which gave little promise of the polished mature beauty which is hers today. Our story was very ordinary. She returned a book to the library one evening when I was on counter duty. We chatted. She asked my advice about novels for her mother. I spent as long as I dared finding suitable romances for her on the shelves. I tried to interest her in the books I liked. I asked her about herself, her life, her ambitions. She was the only woman I had been able to talk to. I was enchanted by her, totally and completely besotted.

I used to take my lunch early and make surreptitious visits to the store, watching her from the shadow of a neighbouring pillar. There is one picture which even now seems to stop my heart. She had dabbed her wrist with scent and was holding out a bare arm over the counter so that a prospective customer could smell the perfume. She was totally absorbed, her young face gravely preoccupied. I watched her, silently, and felt the tears smarting my eyes.

It was a miracle when she agreed to marry me. Her mother (she had no father) was reconciled if not enthusiastic about the match. She didn't, as she made it abundantly plain, consider me much of a catch. But

I had a good job with prospects; I was educated; I was steady and reliable; I spoke with a grammar school accent which, while she affected to deride it, raised my status in her eyes. Besides, any marriage for Elsie was better than none. I was dimly aware when I bothered to think about Elsie in relation to anyone but myself that she and her mother didn't get on.

Mrs Bowman made, as she described it, a splash. There was a full choir and a peal of bells. The church hall was hired and a sit-down meal, ostentatiously unsuitable and badly cooked, was served to eighty guests. Between the pangs of nervousness and indigestion I was conscious of smirking waiters in short white jackets, a couple of giggling bridesmaids from the store, their freckled arms bulging from pink taffeta sleeves, hearty male relatives, red faced and with buttonholes of carnation and waving fern, who made indelicate jokes and clapped me painfully between the shoulders. There were speeches and warm champagne. And, in the middle of it all, Elsie my Elsie, like a white rose.

I suppose that it was stupid of me to imagine that I could hold her. The mere sight of our morning faces, smiling at each other's reflection in the bedroom mirror, should have warned me that it couldn't last.

But, poor deluded fool, I never dreamed that I might lose her except by death. Her death I dared not contemplate, and I was afraid for the first time of my own. Happiness had made a coward of me. We moved into a new bungalow, chosen by Elsie, sat in new chairs chosen by Elsie, slept in a befrilled bed chosen by Elsie. I was so happy that it was like passing into a new phase of existence, breathing a different air, seeing the most ordinary things as if they were newly created. One isn't necessarily humble when greatly in love. Is it so unreasonable to recognize the value of a love like mine, to believe that the beloved is equally sustained and transformed by it?

She said that she wasn't ready to start a baby and, without her job, she was easily bored. She took a brief training in shorthand and typing at our local Technical College and found herself a position as shorthand typist at the firm of Collingford and Major. That, at least, was how the job started. Shorthand typist, then secretary to Mr Rodney Collingford, then personal secretary, then confidential personal secretary; in my bemused state of uxorious bliss I only half registered her progress from occasionally taking his dictation when his then secretary was absent to flaunting his gifts of jewellery and sharing his bed.

He was everything I wasn't. Rich (his father had made a fortune from plastics shortly after the war and had left the factory to his only son), coarsely handsome in a swarthy fashion, big muscled, confident, attractive to women. He prided himself on taking what he wanted. Elsie must have been one of his easiest pickings.

Why, I still wonder, did he want to marry her? I thought at the time that he couldn't resist depriving a pathetic, under-privileged, unattractive husband of a prize which neither looks nor talent had qualified him to deserve. I've noticed that about the rich and success-ful. They can't bear to see the undeserving prosper. I thought that half the satisfaction for him was in taking her away from me. That was partly why I knew that I had to kill him. But now I'm not so sure. I may have done him an injustice. It may have been both simpler and more complicated than that. She was, you see – she still is – so very beautiful.

I understand her better now. She was capable of kindness, good humour, generosity even, provided she was getting what she wanted. At the time we married, and perhaps eighteen months afterwards, she wanted me. Neither her egoism nor her curiosity had been able to resist such a flattering, overwhelming love. But for her, marriage wasn't permanency. It was the first and necessary step towards the kind of life she wanted and meant to have. She was kind to me, in bed and out, while I was what she wanted. But when she wanted someone else, then my need of her, my jealousy, my bitterness, she saw as a cruel and wilful denial of her basic right, the right to have what she wanted. After all, I'd had her for nearly three years. It was two years more than I had any right to expect. She thought so. Her darling Rodney thought so. When my acquaintances at the library learnt of the divorce I could see in their eyes that they thought so too. And she couldn't see what I was so bitter about. Rodney was perfectly happy to be the guilty party; they weren't, she pointed out caustically, expecting me to behave like a gentleman. I wouldn't have to pay for the divorce. Rodney would see to that. I wasn't being asked to provide her with alimony. Rodney had more than enough. At one point she came close to bribing me with Rodney's money to let her go without fuss. And yet – was it really as simple as that? She had loved me, or at least needed me, for a time. Had she perhaps seen in me the father that she had lost at five years old?

During the divorce, through which I was, as it were, gently processed by highly paid legal experts as if I were an embarrassing but expendable nuisance to be got rid of with decent speed, I was only able to keep sane by the knowledge that I was going to kill Collingford. I knew that I couldn't go on living in a world where he breathed the same air. My mind fed voraciously on the thought of his death, savoured it, began systematically and with dreadful pleasure to plan it.

A successful murder depends on knowing your victim, his character, his daily routine, his weaknesses, those unalterable and betraying habits which make up the core of personality. I knew quite a lot about Rodney Collingford. I knew facts which Elsie had let fall in her first weeks with the firm, typing pool gossip. I knew the fuller and rather more intimate facts which she had disclosed in those early days of her enchantment with him, when neither prudence nor kindness had been able to conceal her obsessive preoccupation with her new boss. I should have been warned then. I knew, none better, the need to talk about the absent lover.

What did I know about him? I knew the facts that were common knowledge, of course. That he was wealthy; aged thirty; a notable amateur golfer; that he lived in an ostentatious mock Georgian house on the banks of the Thames looked after by over-paid but non-resident staff; that he owned a cabin cruiser; that he was just over six feet tall; that he was a good business man but reputedly close-fisted; that he was methodical in his habits. I knew a miscellaneous and unrelated set of facts about him, some of which would be useful, some important, some of which I couldn't use. I knew – and this was rather surprising – that he was good with his hands and liked making things in metal and wood. He had built an expensively equipped and large workroom in the grounds of his house and spent every Thursday evening working there alone. He was a man addicted to routine. This creativity, however mundane and trivial, I found intriguing, but I didn't let myself dwell on it. I was interested in him only so far as his personality and habits were relevant to his death. I never thought of him as a human being. He had no existence for me apart from my hate. He was Rodney Collingford, my victim.

First I decided on the weapon. A gun would have been the most certain, I supposed, but I didn't know how to get one and was only too well aware that I wouldn't know how to load or use it if I did. Besides, I was reading a number of books about murder at the time and I realized that guns, however cunningly obtained, were easy to trace. And there was another thing. A gun was too impersonal, too remote. I wanted to make physical contact at the moment of death. I wanted to get close enough to see that final look of incredulity and horror as he recognized, simultaneously, me and his death. I wanted to drive a knife into his throat.

I bought it two days after the divorce. I was in no hurry to kill Collingford. I knew that I must take my time, must be patient, if I were to act in safety. One day, perhaps when we were old, I might tell Elsie. But I didn't intend to be found out. This was to be the perfect murder. And that meant taking my time. He would be allowed to live for a full year. But I knew that the earlier I bought the knife the more difficult it would be, twelve months later, to trace the purchase. I didn't buy it locally. I went one Saturday morning by train and bus to a north-east suburb and found a busy ironmongers and general store just off the High Street. There was a variety of knives on display. The blade of the one I selected was about six inches long and was made of strong steel screwed into a plain wooden handle. I think it was probably meant for cutting lino. In the shop its razor sharp edge was pro-
tected by a strong cardboard sheath. It felt good and

right in my hand. I stood in a small queue at the pay desk and the cashier didn't even glance up as he took my notes and pushed the change towards me.

But the most satisfying part of my planning was the second stage. I wanted Collingford to suffer. I wanted him to know that he was going to die. It wasn't enough that he should realize it in a last second before I drove in the knife or in that final second before he ceased to know anything for ever. Two seconds of agony, however horrible, weren't an adequate return for what he had done to me. I wanted him to know that he was a condemned man, to know it with increasing certainty, to wonder every morning whether this might be his last day. What if this knowledge did make him cautious, put him on his guard? In this country, he couldn't go armed. He couldn't carry on his business with a hired protector always at his side. He couldn't bribe the police to watch him every second of the day. Besides, he wouldn't want to be thought a coward. I guessed that he would carry on, ostentatiously normal, as if the threats were unreal or derisory, something to laugh about with his drinking cronies. He was the sort to laugh at danger. But he would never be sure. And, by the end, his nerve and confidence would be broken. Elsie wouldn't know him for the man she had married. 11

I would have liked to have telephoned him but that, I knew, was impracticable. Calls could be traced; he might refuse to talk to me; I wasn't confident that I could disguise my voice. So the sentence of death would have to be sent by post. Obviously, I couldn't write the notes or the envelopes myself. My studies in murder had shown me how difficult it was to disguise handwriting and the method of cutting out and sticking together letters from a newspaper seemed messy, very time consuming and difficult to manage wearing gloves. I knew, too, that it would be fatal to use my own small portable typewriter or one of the machines at the library. The forensic experts could identify a machine.

And then I hit on my plan. I began to spend my Saturdays and occasional half days journeying round London and visiting shops where they sold second-hand typewriters. I expect you know the kind of shop; a variety of machines of different ages, some practically obsolete, others hardly used, arranged on tables where the prospective purchaser may try them out. There were new machines too, and the proprietor was usually employed in demonstrating their merits or discussing hire purchase terms. The customers wandered desul-

torily around, inspecting the machines, stopping

occasionally to type out an exploratory passage. There were little pads of rough paper stacked ready for use. I didn't, of course, use the scrap paper provided. I came supplied with my own writing materials, a well-known brand sold in every stationer's and on every railway bookstall. I bought a small supply of paper and envelopes once every two months and never from the same shop. Always, when handling them, I wore a thin pair of gloves, slipping them on as soon as my typing was complete. If someone were near, I would tap out the usual drivel about the sharp brown fox or all good men coming to the aid of the party. But if I were quite alone I would type something very different.

'This is the first comunication, Collingford. You'll be getting them regularly from now on. They're just to let you know that I'm going to kill you.'

'You can't escape me, Collingford. Don't bother to inform the police. They can't help you.'

'I'm getting nearer, Collingford. Have you made your will?'

'Not long now, Collingford. What does it feel like to be under sentence of death?'

The warnings weren't particularly elegant. As a librarian I could think of a number of apt quotations which would have added a touch of individuality or style, perhaps even of sardonic humour, to the bald sentence of death. But I dared not risk originality. The notes had to be ordinary, the kind of threat which anyone of his enemies, a worker, a competitor, a cuckolded husband, might have sent.

Sometimes I had a lucky day. The shop would be large, well supplied, nearly empty. I would be able to move from typewriter to typewriter and leave with perhaps a dozen or so notes and addressed envelopes ready to send. I always carried a folded newspaper in which I could conceal my writing pad and envelopes and into which I could quickly slip my little stock of typed messages.

It was quite a job to keep myself supplied with notes and I discovered interesting parts of London and fascinating shops. I particularly enjoyed this part of my plan. I wanted Collingford to get two notes a week, one posted on Sunday and one on Thursday. I wanted him to come to dread Friday and Monday mornings when the familiar typed envelope would drop on his mat. I wanted him to believe the threat was real. And why should he not believe it? How could the force of my hate and resolution not transmit itself through paper and typescript to his gradually comprehending

brain?

I wanted to keep an eye on my victim. It shouldn't have been difficult; we lived in the same town. But our lives were worlds apart. He was a hard and sociable drinker. I never went inside a public house, and would have been particularly ill at ease in the kind of public house he frequented. But, from time to time, I would see him in the town. Usually he would be parking his Jaguar, and I would watch his quick, almost furtive, look to left and right before he turned to lock the door. Was it my imagination that he looked older, that some of the confidence had drained out of him?

Once, when walking by the river on a Sunday in early spring, I saw him manoeuvring his boat through Teddington Lock. Ilsa – she had, I knew, changed her name after her marriage – was with him. She was wearing a white trouser suit, her flowing hair was bound by a red scarf. There was a party. I could see two more men and a couple of girls and hear high female squeals of laughter. I turned quickly and slouched away as if I were the guilty one. But not before I had seen Collingford's face. This time I couldn't be mistaken. It wasn't, surely, the tedious job of getting his boat unscratched through the lock that made his face look so grey and strained.

The third phase of my planning meant moving

house. I wasn't sorry to go. The bungalow, feminine, chintzy, smelling of fresh paint and the new shoddy furniture which she had chosen, was Elsie's home not mine. Her scent still lingered in cupboards and on pillows. In these inappropriate surroundings I had known greater happiness than I was ever to know again. But now I paced restlessly from room to empty room fretting to be gone.

It took me four months to find the house I wanted. It had to be on or very near to the river within two or three miles upstream of Collingford's house. It had to be small and reasonably cheap. Money wasn't too much of a difficulty. It was a time of rising house prices and the modern bungalow sold at three hundred pounds more than I had paid for it. I could get another mortgage without difficulty if I didn't ask for too much, but I thought it likely that, for what I wanted, I should have to pay cash.

The house agents perfectly understood that a man on his own found a three-bedroom bungalow too large for him and, even if they found me rather vague about my new requirements and irritatingly imprecise about the reasons for rejecting their offerings, they still sent me orders to view. And then, suddenly on an afternoon in April, I found exactly what I was looking for. It actually stood on the river, separated from it only by a narrow tow path. It was a one-bedroom shack-like wooden bungalow with a tiled roof, set in a small neglected plot of sodden grass and overgrown flower beds. There had once been a wooden landing stage but now the two remaining planks, festooned with weeds and tags of rotted rope, were half submerged beneath the slime of the river. The paint on the small veranda had long ago flaked away. The wallpaper of twined roses in the sitting-room was blotched and faded. The previous owner had left two old cane chairs and a ramshackle table. The kitchen was pokey and ill-equipped. Everywhere there hung a damp miasma of depression and decay. In summer, when the neighbouring shacks and bungalows were occupied by holidaymakers and week-enders it would, no doubt, be cheerful enough. But in October, when I planned to kill Collingford, it would be as deserted and isolated as a disused morgue. I bought it and paid cash. I was even able to knock two hundred pounds off the asking price.

My life that summer was almost happy. I did my job at the library adequately. I lived alone in the shack, looking after myself as I had before my marriage. I spent my evenings watching television. The images flickered in front of my eyes almost unregarded, a monochrome background to my bloody and obsessive thoughts.

I practised with the knife until it was as familiar in my hand as an eating utensil. Collingford was taller than I by six inches. The thrust then would have to be upward. It made a difference to the way I held the knife and I experimented to find the most comfortable and effective grip. I hung a bolster on a hook in the bedroom door and lunged at a marked spot for hours at a time. Of course, I didn't actually insert the knife; nothing must dull the sharpness of its blade. Once a week, a special treat, I sharpened it to an even keener edge.

Two days after moving into the bungalow I bought a dark blue untrimmed track suit and a pair of light running shoes. Throughout the summer I spent an occasional evening running on the tow path. The people who owned the neighbouring chalets, when they were there which was infrequently, got used to the sound of my television through the closed curtains and the sight of my figure jogging past their windows. I kept apart from them and from everyone and summer passed into autumn. The shutters were put up on all the chalets except mine. The tow path became mushy with falling leaves. Dusk fell early, and the summer sights and sounds died on the river. And it was October.

He was due to die on Thursday October 17th, the anniversary of the final decree of divorce. It had to be a Thursday, the evening which he spent by custom alone in his workshop, but it was a particularly happy augury that the anniversary should fall on a Thursday. I knew that he would be there. Every Thursday for nearly a year I had padded along the two and a half miles of the footpath in the evening dusk and had stood briefly watching the squares of light from his windows and the dark bulk of the house behind.

It was a warm evening. There had been a light drizzle for most of the day but, by dusk, the skies had cleared. There was a thin white sliver of moon and it cast a trembling ribbon of light across the river. I left the library at my usual time, said my usual good-nights. I knew that I had been my normal self during the day, solitary, occasionally a little sarcastic, conscientious, betraying no hint of the inner tumult.

I wasn't hungry when I got home but I made myself eat an omelette and drink two cups of coffee. I put on my swimming trunks and hung around my neck a plastic toilet bag containing the knife. Over the trunks

I put on my track suit, slipping a pair of thin rubber gloves into the pocket. Then, at about quarter past seven, I left the shack and began my customary gentle trot along the tow path.

When I got to the chosen spot opposite to Collingford's house I could see at once that all was well. The house was in darkness but there were the customary lighted windows of his workshop. I saw that the cabin cruiser was moored against the boathouse. I stood very still and listened. There was no sound. Even the light breeze had died and the yellowing leaves on the riverside elms hung motionless. The tow path was completely deserted. I slipped into the shadow of the hedge where the trees grew thickest and found the place I had already selected. I put on the rubber gloves, slipped out of the track suit, and left it folded around my running shoes in the shadow of the hedge. Then, still watching carefully to left and right, I made my way to the river.

I knew just where I must enter and leave the water. I had selected a place where the bank curved gently, where the water was shallow and the bottom was firm and comparatively free of mud. The water struck very cold, but I expected that. Every night during that autumn I had bathed in cold water to accustom my body to the shock. I swam across the river with my methodical but quiet breast stroke, hardly disturbing the dark surface of the water. I tried to keep out of the path of moonlight but, from time to time, I swam into its silver gleam and saw my red gloved hands parting in front of me as if they were already stained with blood.

I used Collingford's landing stage to clamber out the other side. Again I stood still and listened. There was no sound except for the constant moaning of the river and the solitary cry of a night bird. I made my way silently over the grass. Outside the door of his workroom, I paused again. I could hear the noise of some kind of machinery. I wondered whether the door would be locked, but it opened easily when I turned the handle. I moved into a blaze of light.

I knew exactly what I had to do. I was perfectly calm. It was over in about four seconds. I don't think he really had a chance. He was absorbed in what he had been doing, bending over a lathe, and the sight of an almost naked man, walking purposely towards him, left him literally impotent with surprise. But, after that first paralysing second, he knew me. Oh yes, he knew me! Then I drew my right hand from behind my back and struck. The knife went in as sweetly as if the flesh had been butter. He staggered and fell. I had expected that and I let myself go loose and fell on top of him. His eyes were glazed, his mouth opened and there was a gush of dark red blood. I twisted the knife viciously in the wound, relishing the sound of tearing sinews. Then I waited. I counted five deliberately, then raised myself from his supine figure and crouched behind him before withdrawing the knife. When I withdrew it there was a fountain of sweet smelling blood which curved from his throat like an arch. There is one thing I shall never forget. The blood must have been red, what other colour could it have been? But, at the time and for ever afterwards, I saw it as a golden stream.

I checked my body for blood stains before I left the workshop and rinsed my arms under the cold tap at his sink. My bare feet made no marks on the wooden block flooring. I closed the door quietly after me and, once again, stood listening. Still no sound. The house was dark and empty.

The return journey was more exhausting than I had thought possible. The river seemed to have widened and I thought that I should never reach my home shore. I was glad I had chosen a shallow part of the stream and that the bank was firm. I doubt whether I could have drawn myself up through a welter of mud and slime. I was shivering violently as I zipped-up my track suit and it took me precious seconds to get on my running shoes. After I had run about a mile down the tow path I weighted the toilet bag containing the knife with stones from the path and hurled it into the middle of the river. I guessed that they would drag part of the Thames for the weapon but they could hardly search the whole stream. And, even if they did, the toilet bag was one sold at the local chain store which anyone might have bought, and I was confident that the knife could never be traced to me. Half an hour later I was back in my shack. I had left the television on and the news was just ending. I made myself a cup of hot cocoa and sat to watch it. I felt drained of thought and energy as if I had just made love. I was conscious of nothing but my tiredness, my body's coldness gradually returning to life in the warmth of the electric fire, and a great peace.

He must have had quite a lot of enemies. It was nearly a fortnight before the police got round to inter-viewing me. Two officers came, a Detective Inspector and a Sergeant, both in plain clothes. The Sergeant did most of the talking; the other just sat, looking round at the sitting-room, glancing out at the river, 23 looking at the two of us from time to time from cold grey eyes as if the whole investigation were a necessary bore. The Sergeant said the usual reassuring platitudes about just a few questions. I was nervous, but that didn't worry me. They would expect me to be nervous. I told myself that, whatever I did, I mustn't try to be clever. I mustn't talk too much. I had decided to tell them that I spent the whole evening watching television, confident that no one would be able to refute this. I knew that no friends would have called on me. I doubted whether my colleagues at the library even knew where I lived. And I had no telephone so I need not fear that a caller's ring had gone unanswered during that crucial hour and a half.

On the whole it was easier than I had expected. Only once did I feel myself at risk. That was when the Inspector suddenly intervened. He said in a harsh voice:

'He married your wife, didn't he? Took her away from you some people might say. Nice piece of goods, too, by the look of her. Didn't you feel any grievance? Or was it all nice and friendly? You take her, old chap. No ill feelings. That kind of thing.'

It was hard to accept the contempt in his voice but
24 if he hoped to provoke me he didn't succeed. I had

been expecting this question. I was prepared. I looked down at my hands and waited a few seconds before I spoke. I knew exactly what I would say.

'I could have killed Collingford myself when she first told me about him. But I had to come to terms with it. She went for the money you see. And if that's the kind of wife you have, well she's going to leave you sooner or later. Better sooner than when you have a family. You tell yourself "good riddance". I don't mean I felt that at first, of course. But I did feel it in the end. Sooner than I expected, really.'

That was all I said about Elsie then or ever. They came back three times. They asked if they could look round my shack. They looked round it. They took away two of my suits and the track suit for examination. Two weeks later they returned them without comment. I never knew what they suspected, or even if they did suspect. Each time they came I said less, not more. I never varied my story. I never allowed them to provoke me into discussing my marriage or speculating about the crime. I just sat there, telling them the same thing over and over again. I never felt in any real danger. I knew that they had dragged some lengths of the river but that they hadn't found the weapon. In the end they gave up. I always had the feeling that I was pretty low on their list of suspects and that, by the end, their visits were merely a matter of form.

It was three months before Elsie came to me. I was glad that it wasn't earlier. It might have looked suspicious if she had arrived at the shack when the police were with me. After Collingford's death I hadn't seen her. There were pictures of her in the national and local newspapers, fragile in sombre furs and black hat at the inquest, bravely controlled at the crematorium, sitting in her drawing-room in afternoon dress and pearls with her husband's dog at her feet, the personification of loneliness and grief.

'I can't think who could have done it. He must have been a madman. Rodney hadn't an enemy in the world.'

That statement caused some ribald comment at the library. One of the assistants said:

'He's left her a fortune I hear. Lucky for her she had an alibi. She was at a London theatre all the evening, watching *Macbeth*. Otherwise, from what I've heard of our Rodney Collingford, people might have started to get ideas about his fetching little widow.'

Then he gave me a sudden embarrassed glance, remembering who the widow was.

And so one Friday evening, she came. She drove herself and was alone. The dark green Saab drove up at my ramshackle gate. She came into the sitting-room and looked around in a kind of puzzled contempt. After a moment, still not speaking, she sat in one of the fireside chairs and crossed her legs, moving one caressingly against the other. I hadn't seen her sitting like that before. She looked up at me. I was standing stiffly in front of her chair, my lips dry. When I spoke I couldn't recognize my own voice.

'So you've come back?' I said.

She stared at me, incredulous, and then she laughed:

'To you? Back for keeps? Don't be silly, darling! I've just come to pay a visit. Besides, I wouldn't dare to come back, would I? I might be frightened that you'd stick a knife into my throat.'

I couldn't speak. I stared at her, feeling the blood drain from my face. Then I heard her high, rather childish voice. It sounded almost kind.

'Don't worry, I shan't tell. You were right about him, darling, you really were. He wasn't at all nice really. And mean! I didn't care so much about your meanness. After all, you don't earn so very much, do you? But he had half a million! Think of it, darling. I've been left half a million! And he was so mean that 27 he expected me to go on working as his secretary even after we were married. I typed all his letters! I really did! All that he sent from home, anyway. And I had to open his post every morning unless the envelopes had a secret little sign on them he'd told his friends about to show that they were private.'

I said through bloodless lips, 'So all my notes –?'

'He never saw them, darling. Well, I didn't want to worry him, did I? And I knew they were from you. I knew when the first one arrived. You never could spell communication, could you? I noticed that when you used to write to the house agents and the solicitor before we were married. It made me laugh considering that you're an educated librarian and I was only a shop assistant.'

'So you knew all the time. You knew that it was going to happen.'

'Well, I thought that it might. But he really was horrible, darling. You can't imagine. And now I've got half a million! Isn't it lucky that I have an alibi? I thought you might come on that Thursday. And Rodney never did enjoy a serious play.'

After that brief visit I never saw or spoke to her again. I stayed in the shack, but life became pointless after

Collingford's death. Planning his murder had been an interest, after all. Without Elsie and without my victim there seemed little point in living. And, about a year after his death, I began to dream. I still dream, always on a Monday and Friday. I live through it all again; the noiseless run along the tow path over the mush of damp leaves; the quiet swim across the river; the silent opening of his door; the upward thrust of the knife; the vicious turn in the wound; the animal sound of tearing tissues; the curving stream of golden blood. Only the homeward swim is different. In my dream the river is no longer a cleansing stream, luminous under the sickle moon, but a cloying, impenetrable, slow-moving bog of viscous blood through which I struggle in impotent panic towards a steadily receding shore.

I know about the significance of the dream. I've read all about the psychology of guilt. Since I lost Elsie I've done all my living through books. But it doesn't help. And I no longer know who I am. I know who I used to be, our local Assistant Librarian, gentle, scholarly, timid, Elsie's husband. But then I killed Collingford. The man I was couldn't have done that. He wasn't that kind of person. So who am I? It isn't really surprising, I suppose, that the Library Committee suggested so tactfully that I ought to look for a less exacting job. A less exacting job than the post of Assistant Librarian? But you can't blame them. No one can be efficient and keep his mind on the job when he doesn't know who he is.

Sometimes, when I'm in a public house – and I seem to spend most of my time there nowadays since I've been out of work – I'll look over someone's shoulder at a newspaper photograph of Elsie and say:

'That's the beautiful Ilsa Mancelli. I was her first husband.'

I've got used to the way people sidle away from me, the ubiquitous pub bore, their eyes averted, their voices suddenly hearty. But sometimes, perhaps because they've been lucky with the horses and feel a spasm of pity for a poor deluded sod, they push a few coins over the counter to the barman before making their way to the door, and buy me a drink.

The Girl Who Loved Graveyards

She couldn't remember anything about that day in the hot August of 1956 when they took her to live with her Aunt Gladys and Uncle Victor in the small house in east London, at 49 Alma Terrace. She knew that it was three days after her tenth birthday and that she was to be cared for by her only living relations now that her father and grandmother were dead, killed by influenza within a week of each other. But those were just facts someone, at some time, had told her briefly. She could remember nothing of her previous life. Those first ten years were a void, unsubstantial as a dream that had faded but that had left on her mind a scar of unarticulated childish anxiety and fear. For her, memory and childhood both began with that moment when, waking in the small, unfamiliar bedroom with the kitten, Blackie, still curled up asleep on a towel at the foot of her bed, she had walked barefoot to the window and drawn back the curtain. And there, stretched beneath her, lay the cemetery, luminous and mysterious in the early morning light, bounded by iron railings and separated from the rear of Alma Terrace only by a narrow path. It was to be another warm day, and over the serried rows of headstones lay a thin haze pierced by the occasional obelisk and by the wing tips of marble angels whose disembodied heads seemed to be floating on particles of shimmering light. And as she watched, motionless in an absorbed enchantment, the mist began to rise and the whole cemetery was revealed to her, a miracle of stone and marble, bright grass and summer-laden trees, flower-bedecked graves and intersecting paths stretching as far as the eye could see. In the distance she could just make out the spire of a Victorian chapel, gleaming like the spire of some magical castle in a long-forgotten fairy tale. In those moments of growing wonder she found herself shivering with delight, an emotion so rare that it stole through her thin body like a pain. And it was then, on the first morning of her new life, with the past a void and the future unknown and frightening, that she made the cemetery her own. Throughout her childhood and youth it was to remain a place of delight and mystery, her refuge and her solace.

It was a childhood without love, almost without affection. Her uncle Victor was her father's elder half-brother; that too she had been told. He and her aunt weren't really her relations. Their small capacity for love was expended on each other, and even here it was less a positive emotion than a pact of mutual support and comfort against the threatening world that lay outside the trim curtains of their small, claustrophobic sitting-room.

But they cared for her as dutifully as she cared for the cat Blackie. It was a fiction in the household that she adored Blackie, her own cat, brought with her when she arrived, her one link with the past, almost her only possession. Only she knew that she disliked and feared him. But she brushed and fed him with conscientious care as she did everything, and in return he gave her a slavish allegiance, hardly ever leaving her side, slinking through the cemetery at her heels and turning back only when they reached the main gate. But he wasn't her friend. He didn't love her and he knew she didn't love him. He was a fellow conspirator, gazing at her through slits of azure light, relishing some secret knowledge that was her knowledge too. He ate voraciously, yet he never grew fat. Instead his sleek black body lengthened until, stretched in the sunlight along her windowsill, his sharp nose turned always to the cemetery, he looked as sinister and unnatural as a furred reptile.

It was lucky for her that there was a side gate to the cemetery from Alma Terrace and that she could take a shortcut to and from school across the graveyard, avoiding the dangers of the main road. On her first morning her uncle had said doubtfully, 'I suppose it's all right. But it seems wrong, somehow, a child walking every day through rows of the dead.'

Her aunt had replied: 'The dead can't rise from their graves. They lie quiet. She's safe enough from the dead.' Her voice had been unnaturally gruff and loud. The words had sounded like an assertion, almost a defiance. But the child knew her aunt was right. She did feel safe with the dead – safe and at home.

The years in Alma Terrace slipped by, as bland and dull as her aunt's blancmange, a sensation rather than a taste. Was she happy? That was a question it had never occurred to her to ask. She wasn't unpopular at school, being neither pretty nor intelligent enough to provoke much interest either from the children or the staff; an ordinary child, unusual only in that she was an orphan, but unable to capitalize even on that sentimental advantage. Perhaps she might have found friends, quiet, unenterprising children like her, who would respond to her unthreatening mediocrity, but something about her repelled their timid advances: her self-sufficiency, the bland, uncaring gaze, the refusal to give anything of herself even in casual friendship. She didn't need friends. She had the graveyard and its occupants.

She had her favourites. She knew them all – when they had died, how old they had been, sometimes how they had died. She knew their names and learned their memorials by heart. They were more real to her than the living, those rows of dearly loved wives and mothers, respected tradesmen, lamented fathers, deeply mourned children.

The new graves hardly ever interested her, although she would watch the funerals from a distance and creep up later to read the mourning cards. What she liked best were the old, neglected oblongs of mounded earth or chipped stones, the tilted crosses, the carved words almost erased by time. It was around the names of the long dead that she wove her childish fantasies.

Even the seasons of the year she experienced in and through the cemetery. The gold and purple spears of the first crocuses thrusting through the hard earth. April with its tossing daffodils. The whole graveyard *en fête* in yellow and white as mourners dressed the graves for Easter. The smell of mown grass and the earthy tang of high summer, as if the dead were breathing the flower-scented air and exuding their own mysterious miasma. The glare of sunlight on stone and marble as the old women in their stained cotton dresses shuffled with their vases to fill them at the tap behind the chapel. Seeing the cemetery transformed by the first snow of winter, the marble angels grotesque in their high bonnets of glistening snow. Watching at her window for the thaw, hoping to catch that moment when the edifice would slip and the shrouded shapes become themselves again.

Only once had she asked about her father, and then she had known, as children do, that this was a subject which, for some mysterious adult reason, it was better not to talk about. She had been sitting at the kitchen table with her homework while her aunt was busy cooking supper. Looking up from her history book, she asked: 'Where is Daddy buried?'

The frying pan clattered against the stove. The cooking fork dropped from her aunt's hand. It took her a long time to pick it up, wash it, clean the grease from the floor. The child asked once again: 'Where is Daddy buried?'

'Up north. At Creedon, outside Nottingham, with your mum and gran. Where else?'

'Can I go there? Can I visit him?'

'When you're older, maybe. No sense, is there, hanging about graves? The dead aren't there.'

'Who looks after them?'

'The graves? The cemetery people. Now get on with your homework.'

She hadn't asked about her mother, the mother who died when she was born. That desertion had always seemed to her wilful, a source of secret guilt. 'You killed your mother.' Someone sometime had spoken those words to her, had laid on her that burden. She wouldn't let herself think about her mother. But she knew that her father had stayed with her, had loved her, hadn't wanted to die and leave her. Someday, secretly, she would find his grave. She would visit it, not once, but every week. She would tend it and plant flowers on it and clip the grass as the old ladies did in the cemetery. And if there wasn't a stone, she would pay for one, bearing his name and an epitaph she would choose. She would have to wait until she was older, until she could leave school and go to work and save enough money. But one day she would find her father. She would have a grave of her own to visit and tend. There was a debt of love to be paid.

Four years after her arrival in Alma Terrace, her aunt's only brother came to visit from Australia. Physically he and his sister were alike, the same stolid, short-legged bodies, the same small eyes set in square, pudgy faces. But Uncle Ned had a brash assurance, a cheerful geniality that was so alien to his sister's unconfident reserve that it was hard to believe they were siblings. For two weeks he dominated the little house with his strident, alien voice and assertive masculinity. There were unfamiliar treats, dinners in the West End, a show at Earl's Court. He was kind to the child, tipping her lavishly, even walking through the cemetery with her one morning on his way to buy his racing paper. And it was that evening, coming silently down the stairs to supper, that she overheard disjointed scraps of conversation, adult talk, incomprehensible at the time but taken into her mind and stored there.

First the harsh boom of her uncle's voice: 'We were looking at this gravestone together, see. "Beloved husband and father. Taken from us suddenly on 14 March 1892." Something like that. Marble chips, cracked urn, bloody great angel pointing upward. You know the kind of thing. Then the kid turned to me, "Daddy's death was sudden too." That's what she said. Came out with it cool as you please. Now, what in God's name made her say that? It gave me a turn, I can tell you. I didn't know where to put my face. And what a place to choose, the bloody cemetery. I'll say one thing for coming out to St Kilda – you'll get a better view. I can promise you that.'

Creeping closer, she strained her ears vainly to catch the indistinct mutter of her aunt's reply. Then came her uncle's voice again: 'That old bitch never forgave him for getting Helen pregnant.

'No one was good enough for her precious only daughter. And then when Helen died having the kid, she blamed him for that too. Poor sod, Sidney bought a packet of trouble when he set eyes on that girl.'

Again the murmur of indistinguishable voices, the sound of her aunt's footsteps moving from table to stove, the scrape of a chair. Then her Uncle Ned's voice again: 'Funny kid, isn't she? Old-fashioned. Morbid, you might say. Seems to live in that bone-yard, she and that damned cat. And the spitting image of her dad.

'It turned me up, I can tell you. Looking at me with his eyes and then coming out with it: "Daddy's death was sudden too." I'll say it was! Helps having such an ordinary name, I suppose. People don't catch on. How long ago? Four years? It seems longer.'

Only one part of this half-heard, incomprehensible conversation had disturbed her. Uncle Ned was trying to persuade them to join him in Australia. She might be taken away from Alma Terrace, might never see the cemetery again, might have to wait for years before she could save enough money to return to England and find her father's grave. And how could she visit it regularly, how could she tend and care for it, from the other side of the world? After Uncle Ned's visit ended, it was months before she could see one of his rare letters with the Australian stamp drop through the letterbox without feeling the cold clutch of fear at her heart.

She needn't have worried. It was October of 1966 before they left England, and they went alone. When they broke the news to her one Sunday morning at breakfast, it was apparent that they had never even considered taking her with them. Dutiful as ever, they had waited to make their decision until she had left school and was earning her living as a shorthand typist with a local firm of estate agents. Her future was assured. They had done all that conscience required of them. Hesitant and a little shamefaced, they justified their decision as if they believed that it was important to her. Her aunt's arthritis was increasingly troublesome; they longed for the sun; Uncle Ned was their only close relation and none of them was getting any younger. Their plan, over which they had agonized for months in whispers behind closed doors, was to visit St Kilda for six months and then, if they liked Australia, to apply to emigrate. The house in Alma Terrace was to be sold to pay the air fare. It was already on the market. But they had made provision for her. When they told her what had been arranged, she had to bend her face low over her plate lest the flood of joy be too apparent. Mrs Morgan, three doors down, would be glad to take her as a lodger if she didn't mind having the small bedroom at the back overlooking the cemetery. In the surging tumult of relief she hardly heard her aunt's next words. Everyone knew how Mrs Morgan was about cats. Blackie would have to be put to sleep.

She was to move into 43 Alma Terrace on the afternoon of the day on which her aunt and uncle flew from Heathrow. Her two cases, holding all that she possessed in the world, were already packed. In her handbag she carefully stowed the meagre official confirmations of her existence: her birth certificate, her medical card, her Post Office savings book showing the £103 painstakingly saved towards the cost of her father's memorial. The next day, she would begin her search. But first she took Blackie to the veterinarian to be destroyed. She had made a cat box and sat patiently in the waiting room with the box at her feet. The cat made no sound, and this patient resignation touched her, evoking for the first time a spasm of pity and affection. But there was nothing she could do to save him. They both knew it. But then it seemed he had always known what she was thinking, what was past and what was to come. There was something they shared, some knowledge, some common experience she couldn't remember and he couldn't express. Now, with his destruction, even that tenuous link with her first ten years would go forever.

When it was her turn to go into the surgery she said, 'I want him put to sleep.'

The veterinarian passed his strong, experienced hands over the sleek fur. 'Are you sure? He seems healthy still. He's old, of course, but in remarkably good condition.'

'I'm sure. I want him put to sleep.' And she left him there without a glance or another word.

She had thought that she would be glad to be free of the pretence of loving him, free of those slitted, accusing eyes. But as she walked back to Alma Terrace she found herself crying: tears, unbidden and unstoppable, ran like rain down her face.

There was no difficulty in getting a week's leave from her job; she had been husbanding her holiday entitlement. Her work, as always, was up to date. She had calculated how much money she would need for her train and bus fares and for a week's stay in modest hotels. Her plans had been made. They had been made for years. She would begin her search with the address on her birth certificate – Cranstoun House, Creedon, Nottingham, the house where she was born. The present owners might remember her father and her. If not, there would be neighbours or older inhabitants of the village who would be able to recall her father's death, where he was buried. If that failed, she would try the local undertakers. It was, after all, only ten years ago. Someone would remember. Somewhere in Nottingham there would be a record of burials. She told Mrs Morgan that she was taking a week's holiday to visit her father's old home, packed a holdall with necessities and next morning caught the earliest possible train to Nottingham.

It was during the bus ride from Nottingham to Creedon that she felt the first stirrings of anxiety and mistrust. Until then she had travelled in calm confidence, but strangely without excitement, as if this long-planned journey were as natural and inevitable as her daily walk to work, an inescapable pilgrimage ordained from that moment when a barefoot child in her white nightdress drew back her bedroom curtains and saw her kingdom spread beneath her. But now her mood changed. As the bus lurched through the suburbs she found herself shifting in her seat as if mental unease were provoking physical discomfort. She had expected green countryside, small churches guarding neat, domestic graveyards patterned with yew trees. These were graveyards she had visited on holidays, had loved almost as much as she loved the one she had made her own. Surely it was in such bird-loud, sanctified peace that her father lay. But Nottingham had spread out during the past ten years, and Creedon was now little more than an urban village separated from the city by a ribbon development of brash new houses, petrol stations and parades of shops. Nothing was familiar, and yet she knew that she had travelled this road before and travelled it in anxiety and pain.

When, 30 minutes later, the bus stopped at its terminus at Creedon, she knew at once where she was.

44 The Dog and Whistle still stood at one corner of the

dusty, litter-strewn village green with the same bus shelter outside it. And at the sight of its graffiti-scrawled walls, memory returned as if nothing had ever been forgotten. Here her father used to leave her when he brought her to pay her regular Sunday visits to her grandmother. Here her grandmother's elderly cook would be waiting for her. Here she would look back for a final wave and see her father patiently waiting for the bus to begin its return journey. Here she would be brought at 6.30, when he arrived to collect her. Cranstoun House was where her grandmother lived. She herself had been born there but it had never been her home.

She had no need to ask her way to the house. And when, five minutes later, she stood gazing up at it in appalled fascination, no need to read the name painted on the shabby, padlocked gate. It was a square-built home of dark brick standing in incongruous and spurious grandeur at the end of a country lane. It was smaller than she remembered, but it was still a dreadful house. How could she ever have forgotten those ornate overhanging gables, the high-pitched roof, the secretive oriel windows, the single forbidding turret at the east end? There was an estate agent's board wired to the gate; the house itself was empty. The paint on the front door was peeling, the lawns were overgrown, the boughs of the rhododendron bushes were broken and the gravel path was studded with weeds. There was no one here who could help her to find her father's grave. But she knew that she had to visit, had to make herself pass again through that intimidating front door. There was something the house knew and had to tell her, something Blackie had known. She couldn't escape her next step. She must find the estate agent's office and get a permit to view.

She had missed the returning bus, and by the time the next one had reached Nottingham, it was after 3.00. Although she had eaten nothing since her early breakfast, she was too driven now to be aware of hunger. But she knew that it would be a long day and that she ought to eat. She turned into a coffee bar and had a toasted cheese sandwich and a mug of coffee, grudging the few minutes it took to gulp them down. The coffee was hot and almost tasteless, but she realised as the hot liquid stung her throat how much she had needed it.

The girl at the cash desk was able to direct her to the house agent's office, a ten minutes' walk away. She was received by a sharp-featured young man in a
pinstripe suit who, after one practised glance at her old

blue tweed coat, the cheap holdall and bag of synthetic leather, placed her precisely in his private category of client from whom little could be expected and to whom less needed to be given. But he found the particulars for her, and his curiosity sharpened as she merely glanced at them and then folded the paper away in her bag. Her request to view that afternoon was received, as she had expected, with politeness but without enthusiasm. But this was familiar territory and she knew why. The house was unoccupied. She would have to be escorted. There was nothing in her respectable drabness to suggest that she was a likely purchaser. And when he briefly excused himself to consult a colleague and returned to say that he would drive her to Creedon at once, she knew the probable reason for that too. The office wasn't busy and it was time that someone from the firm checked up on the property.

Neither of them spoke during the drive. When they reached Creedon and he turned down the lane to the house, the apprehension she had felt on her first visit returned, only it was deeper and stronger. Now it was more than the memory of an old wretchedness. This was childhood misery and fear relived, and intensified by a dreadful adult foreboding. The house agent parked his Morris on the grassy verge, and as she 47 looked up at the blind windows she was seized by a spasm of terror so acute that momentarily she was unable to speak or move. She was aware of the man's holding open the door for her, of the smell of beer on his breath, of his face, uncomfortably close, bending on her a look of exasperated patience. She wanted to say that she had changed her mind, that the house was totally wrong for her, that there would be no point in viewing it, that she would wait for him in the car. But she willed herself to rise from the warm seat and scrambled out under his supercilious eyes. She waited in silence as he unlocked the padlock and swung open the gate.

They passed together between the neglected lawns and the spreading rhododendron bushes toward the front door. And suddenly the feet shuffling on the gravel beside her were different feet and she knew that she was walking with her father as she had walked in childhood. She had only to stretch out her hand to feel the grasp of his fingers. Her companion was saying something about the house but she didn't hear. The meaningless chatter faded and she heard a different voice, her father's voice, heard for the first time in over ten years: 'It won't be for always, darling. Just until I've found a job. And I'll visit you every Sunday for lunch. Afterwards we'll be able to go for a walk together, just the two of us. Grannie has promised that. And I'll buy you a kitten. I'm sure Grannie won't mind when she sees him. A black kitten. You've always wanted a black kitten. What shall we call him? Little Blackie? He'll remind you of me. And then when I've found a job, I'll be able to rent a little house and we'll be together again. I'll look after you, my darling. We'll look after each other.'

She dared not look up lest she see again those desperately pleading eyes begging her to understand, to make things easy for him, not to despise him. She knew now that she ought to have helped him, to have told him that she understood, that she didn't mind living with Grannie for a month or so, that everything would be all right. But she hadn't managed so adult a response. She remembered tears, desperate clinging to his coat, her grandmother's old cook, tight-lipped, pulling her away from him and bearing her up to bed. And the last memory was of watching him from her room above the porch, of his drooping, defeated figure making its way down the lane to the bus stop.

As they reached the front door she looked up. The window was still there. Of course it was. She knew every room in this dark house.

The garden was bathed in a mellow October sunlight; yet the hall struck cold and dim. The heavy mahogany staircase led up from gloom to a darkness which hung above them like a weight. The estate agent felt along the wall for the light switch. She didn't wait. She felt again the huge brass doorknob that her childish fingers had hardly encompassed and moved unerringly into the drawing room. The smell of the room was different. Then there had been a scent of violets overlaid with furniture polish. Now the air smelled cold and musty. She stood in the darkness, shivering but perfectly calm. It seemed to her that she had passed through a barrier of fear as a tortured victim might pass through a pain barrier into a kind of peace. She felt a shoulder brush against her as the man went across to the window and swung open the heavy curtains.

He said, 'The last owners have left it partly furnished. Looks better that way. Easier to get offers if the place looks lived in.'

'Has there been an offer?'

'Not yet. It's not everyone's cup of tea. Bit on the large side for a modern family. Then too, there's the murder. Ten years ago, but people still talk. There've been four owners since, and none of them stayed long.

It's bound to affect the price. No good thinking you can hush up murder.'

His voice was carefully nonchalant but his gaze never left her face. Walking to the empty firegrate, he stretched one arm along the mantelpiece and followed her with his eyes as she moved trance-like about the room.

She heard herself asking: 'What murder?'

'A 64-year-old woman. Battered to death by her son-in-law. The old cook came in from the back kitchen and found him with the poker in his hand. Come to think of it, it could have been one like that.'

He nodded at the collection of brass fire irons resting against the fender. He said, 'It happened right where you're standing now. She was sitting in that very chair.'

She said in a voice so gruff and harsh that she hardly recognized it: 'It wasn't this chair. It was bigger. Her chair had an embroidered seat and back and there were armrests edged with crochet and the feet were like lions' claws.'

His gaze sharpened. Then he laughed warily. The watchful eyes grew puzzled, then the look changed into something else. Could it have been contempt?

'So you know about it. You're one of those.'

'One of those?'

'You aren't really in the market for a place. Couldn't afford one this size anyway. You just want a thrill, want to see where it happened. You get all sorts in this game and I can usually tell. I can give you all the gory details you're interested in. Not that there was much gore. The skull was smashed but most of the bleeding was internal. They say there was just a trickle falling down her forehead and dripping on to her hands.'

It came out so pat that she knew he had told it all before, he enjoyed telling it, this small recital of horror to titillate his clients and relieve the boredom of his day. She wished she weren't so cold. If only she could get warm again, her voice wouldn't sound so strange. She said through her dry lips: 'And the kitten. Tell me about the kitten.'

'Now, that was something! That was a touch of horror. The kitten was on her lap, licking up the blood. But then, you know, don't you. You've heard all about it.'

'Yes,' she lied. 'I heard all about it.' But she had done more than that. She knew. She had seen it. She had been there.

And then the outline of the chair before her altered. An amorphous black shape swam before her eyes; then it took form and substance. Her grandmother was sitting there, squat as a toad, dressed in her Sunday black for morning service, gloved and hatted, prayer book in her lap. She saw again the glob of phlegm at the corner of the mouth, the thread of broken veins at the side of the sharp nose. The grandmother was waiting to inspect her grandchild before church, turning on her again that look of querulous discontent. The witch was sitting there. The witch who hated her and her Daddy, who had told her that he was useless and feckless and no better than her mother's murderer. The witch who was threatening to have Blackie put to sleep because he had torn her chair, because Daddy had given him to her. The witch who was planning to keep her from Daddy forever. And then she saw something else. The poker was there too, just as she remembered it, the long rod of polished brass with its heavy knob.

She seized it now as she had seized it then, and with a high scream of hatred and terror, brought it down on her grandmother's head. Again and again she struck, hearing the brass thudding against the leather, blow on splitting blow. And still she screamed. The room rang with the terror of it. But it was only when the frenzy passed and the dreadful noise stopped that she knew from the pain of her throat that the screaming had been hers.

She stood shaking, gasping for breath. Beads of sweat stood out on her forehead and she felt the stinging drops seeping into her eyes. Looking up, she was aware of the estate man's eyes, wide with terror, staring into hers, of a muttered curse, of footsteps running to the door. And then the poker slid from her moist hands and she heard it thud softly on the rug.

He had been right; there was no blood. Only the grotesque hat knocked forward over the dead face. But while she watched, a sluggish line of deep red rolled from under the brim, zigzagged down the forehead, trickled along the creases of the cheeks and began to drop steadily on to the gloved hands. And then she heard a soft mew. A ball of black fur crept from behind the chair and the ghost of Blackie, azure eyes frantic, leaped, as he had leaped ten years earlier, delicately into that unmoving lap. She looked at her hands. Where were the gloves, the white cotton gloves that the witch had always insisted must be worn to church? But these hands, no longer the hands of a nine-year-old child, were naked. And the chair was empty. There was nothing but the split leather, the burst of horsehair stuffing, a faint smell of violets fading on the quiet air.

She walked out the front door without closing it behind her as she had left it then. She walked as she had walked then, gloved and unsullied, down the gravel path between the rhododendrons, through the ironwork gate and up the lane towards the church. The bell had only just started ringing: she would be in good time. In the distance she had glimpsed her father climbing a stile from the water meadow into the lane. So he must have set out early after breakfast and had walked to Creedon. And why so early? Had he needed that long walk to settle something in his mind? Had it been a pathetic attempt to propitiate the witch by coming with them to church? Or – blessed thought – had he come to take her away, to see that her few belongings were packed and ready by the time the service was over? Yes, that was what she had thought at the time. She remembered it now, that fountain of hope soaring and dancing into glorious certainty. When she got home, all would be ready. They would stand there together and defy the witch, would tell her that they were leaving together, the two of them and Blackie, that she would never see them again. At the end of the road she looked back and saw for the last time the beloved ghost, crossing the lane to the house toward that fatally open door.

And after that? The vision was fading now. She could remember nothing of the service except a blaze of red and blue shifting like a kaleidoscope, then fusing into a stained-glass window, the Good Shepherd gathering a lamb to his bosom. And afterwards? Surely there had been strangers waiting on the porch, grave, concerned faces, whispers and sidelong glances, a woman in some kind of uniform, an official car. And after that, nothing. Memory was a blank. But now at last she knew where her father was buried. And she knew why she would never be able to visit him, never make that pious pilgrimage to the place where he lay because of her, the shameful place where she had put him. There could be no flowers, no obelisk, no loving message carved in marble for those who lay in quick-lime behind a prison wall. And then, unbidden, came the final memory. She saw again the open church door, the trickle of congregation filing in, inquiring faces turning toward her as she arrived alone in the vestibule. She heard again that high, childish voice speaking the words that more than any others had slipped the

rope of hemp over his shrouded head.

'Granny? She isn't very well. She told me to come on my own. No, there's nothing to worry about. She's quite all right. Daddy's with her.'

PENGUIN 60s

ISABEL ALLENDE · *Voices in My Ear*

NICHOLSON BAKER · *Playing Trombone*

LINDSEY BAREHAM · *The Little Book of Big Soups*

KAREN BLIXEN · *From the Ngong Hills*

DIRK BOGARDE · *Coming of Age*

ANTHONY BURGESS · *Childhood*

ANGELA CARTER · *Lizzie Borden*

CARLOS CASTANEDA · *The Sorcerer's Ring of Power*

ELIZABETH DAVID · *Peperonata and Other Italian Dishes*

RICHARD DAWKINS · *The Pocket Watchmaker*

GERALD DURRELL · *The Pageant of Fireflies*

RICHARD ELLMANN · *The Trial of Oscar Wilde*

EPICURUS · *Letter on Happiness*

MARIANNE FAITHFULL · *Year One*

KEITH FLOYD · *Hot and Spicy Floyd*

ALEXANDER FRATER · *Where the Dawn Comes Up like Thunder*

ESTHER FREUD · *Meeting Bilal*

JOHN KENNETH GALBRAITH · *The Culture of Contentment*

ROB GRANT AND DOUG NAYLOR · *Scenes from the Dwarf*

ROBERT GRAVES · *The Gods of Olympus*

JANE GRIGSON · *Puddings*

SOPHIE GRIGSON · *From Sophie's Table*

KATHARINE HEPBURN · *Little Me*

JAMES HERRIOT · *Seven Yorkshire Tales*

SUSAN HILL · *The Badness within Him*

ALAN HOLLINGHURST · *Adventures Underground*

BARRY HUMPHRIES · *Less is More Please*

HOWARD JACOBSON · *Expulsion from Paradise*

P. D. JAMES · *The Girl Who Loved Graveyards*

STEPHEN KING · *Umney's Last Case*